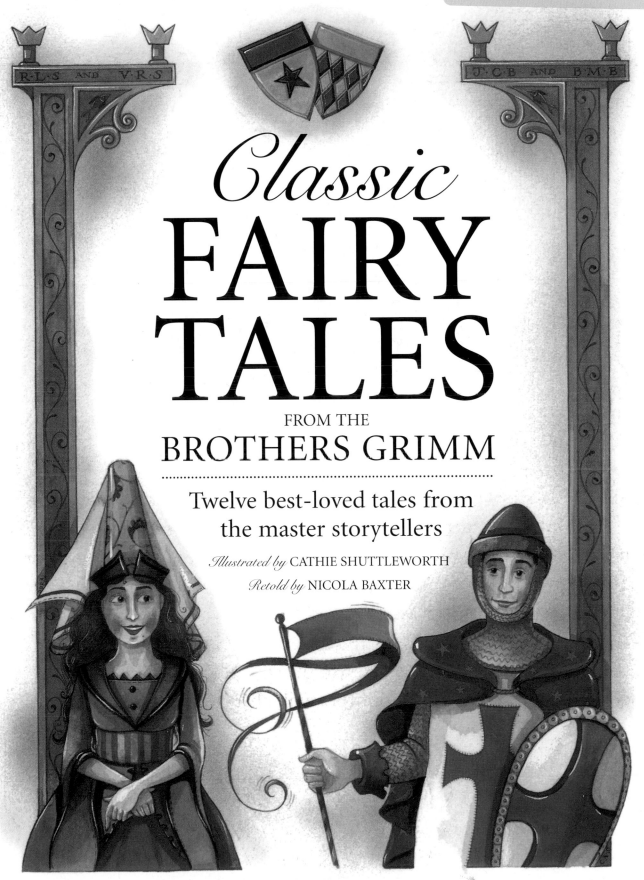

Classic FAIRY TALES

FROM THE
BROTHERS GRIMM

Twelve best-loved tales from
the master storytellers

Illustrated by CATHIE SHUTTLEWORTH

Retold by NICOLA BAXTER

ARMADILLO

This edition is published by Armadillo, an imprint of Anness Publishing Ltd,
Blaby Road, Wigston, Leicestershire LE18 4SE; info@anness.com

www.annesspublishing.com

If you like the images in this book and would like to investigate using them for
publishing, promotions or advertising, please visit our website www.practicalpictures.com
for more information.

Publisher: Joanna Lorenz
Produced by Nicola Baxter
Editorial consultant: Ronne Randall
Designer: Amanda Hawkes
Production controller: Don Campaniello

ETHICAL TRADING POLICY
Trees are being cultivated to replace the materials used to make this product. For further
information about our ecological investment scheme, go to www.annesspublishing.com/trees

PUBLISHER'S NOTE
The author and publishers have made every effort to ensure that this book is safe for its
intended use, and cannot accept any legal responsibility or liability for any harm or injury
arising from misuse.

Manufacturer: Anness Publishing Ltd, Blaby Road, Wigston, Leicestershire LE18 4SE, England
For Product Tracking go to: www.annesspublishing.com/tracking
Batch: 6049-20925-1127

Classic FAIRY TALES

FROM THE
BROTHERS GRIMM

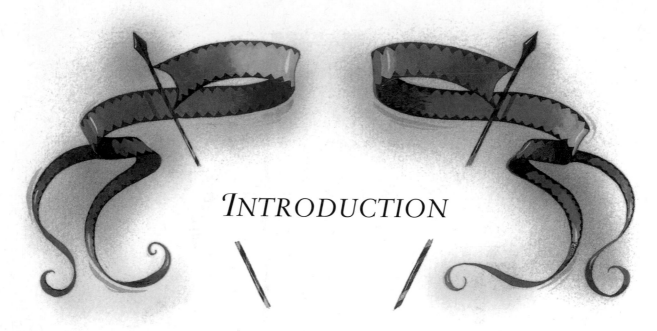

INTRODUCTION

Jacob Ludwig Carl Grimm was born in 1785 in Germany. His brother Wilhelm Carl came along a year later. Both brothers loved the German language and the stories that were told in it. In 1812, they published their first anthology of folk and fairy tales, collected from all over Germany. Many of the stories had been told for centuries, enchanting children and adults with their mixture of magic, mystery and truths older even than the stories themselves.

Each time a story is told, it changes a little, to suit its teller and its audience. Everyone has a different idea about why the characters act as they do and which part of the story is most interesting. So these stories are not *exactly* as the Brothers Grimm heard them, two hundred years ago and in a different language, but they are still full of strange and wonderful things. When you tell them to your own children, no doubt they will change a little more.

Pictures tell stories too from age to age;
Search if you wish
And find a fish
Swimming on every page.

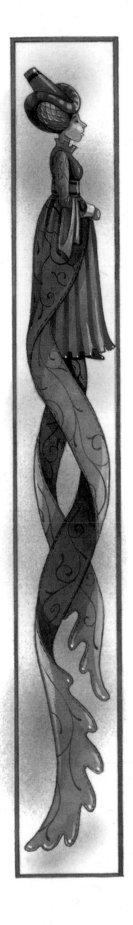

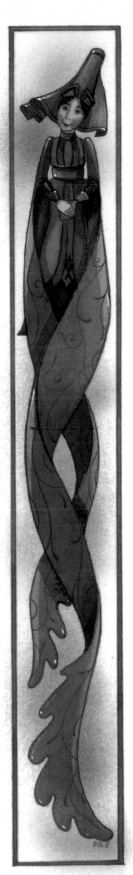

CONTENTS

HANSEL AND GRETEL

There was once a woodcutter whose beloved wife died, leaving him to bring up two little children. After a while, the woodcutter married again, but soon after that times became hard, and there was often not enough to eat in the woodcutter's cottage.

The new wife tried to make ends meet, but she soon became tired and sad. One evening, when the children were in bed, she spoke to the woodcutter.

"We do not have enough food for all four of us. Let's take the children into the forest and leave them there. Who knows, someone who will be able to take care of them better than we can may find them."

The woodcutter did not want to agree, but he could not think of another solution. Meanwhile, the woodcutter's children had been listening at the door.

"Don't worry, Gretel," said the little boy, whose name was Hansel. "I know how we can find our way home again."

The next day, the family went deep into the forest. As they walked, Hansel dropped crumbs from the crust of bread that he had saved for his lunch, hoping to follow them back home again. But the birds soon ate the crumbs, and when the children were left all alone in the forest, they were completely lost.

Hungry and afraid, Hansel and Gretel wandered through the trees. Suddenly, they saw a wonderful sight! A cottage made of candy and gingerbread!

But no sooner had the children munched into the house, than a sharp voice shouted from the window.

"Eat your fill, dear children, but you will pay for every bite. Ha, ha, ha!"

Before they knew what was happening, the children were bundled into the house by the witch who lived there.

"You will work for me, sweetheart," she said to Gretel, "but your dear brother will be a tasty dinner when he is a little fatter."

Every day the witch, whose eyesight was very poor, would ask Hansel to poke his finger out of the cage where she kept him, so that she could see if he was fat enough to eat. Hansel held out a chicken bone to make her think that he was still just skin and bones himself.

At last the day came when the witch could wait no longer.

"Stoke up the fire, sweetheart," she said to Gretel, "and put your head in the oven to see if it is hot enough."

But Gretel did not trust the old witch.

"I don't know," she said. "You'd better check yourself."

No sooner had the witch poked her head in the oven, than Gretel gave her a huge push and slammed the door shut. Then she hurried to free Hansel.

Gathering up the witch's treasures, the children ran from the house, but they did not know which way to turn.

"Oh look!" said Hansel, suddenly. "It's one of the little birds that ate my crumbs. She is going to show us the way!"

The woodcutter could hardly believe his eyes when he saw his children returning. His wife had left, and he was all alone. When he saw the treasure that Hansel and Gretel had taken from the witch's house, the woodcutter laughed.

"This will make us comfortable for the rest of our lives," he said. "But you two are my real treasure, and I will never lose you again."

SLEEPING BEAUTY

Once there lived a King and a Queen who had no children. When, at last, a baby daughter was born to them, they were overjoyed.

"I shall give the biggest and best feast ever seen for her," said her proud father.

It seemed as though everyone in the kingdom was invited. The most important guests were the twelve fairies who make special wishes for children. In fact, there were thirteen fairies in the kingdom, but in his excitement, the King forgot to invite the last one.

At the feast, the twelve fairies gave the little girl their best gifts: beauty and riches and goodness and much more.

Just as the eleventh fairy had finished her wish, there was a crash as the great door swung open. It was the thirteenth fairy!

"So you felt you didn't need me!" she screeched. "Here's *my* present! On her fifteenth birthday, the Princess will prick her finger on a spindle and die!" And she swept from the glittering room, as a terrible silence fell.

As the guests looked at each other in horror, the twelfth fairy spoke.

"I cannot take away the curse completely," she said, "but I can make it better. The Princess *will* prick her finger, but she will not die. Instead, she will fall asleep for a hundred years."

The years passed, as years do, and the Princess grew up to be clever and kind and beautiful, just as the fairies had promised. On the morning of her fifteenth birthday, she woke up early and walked out into the castle courtyard.

It was a beautiful day. As she walked, the Princess suddenly saw the sunlight glinting on a little door that she had never noticed before. She opened it and climbed eagerly up the winding stairs inside.

At the top of the stairs was an open door, through which a very old woman could be seen as she sat, spinning.

Now the Princess had never seen anyone spinning before, for the King had banished all spindles from the kingdom when he heard the thirteenth fairy's curse.

"What are you doing, good woman?" asked the Princess, politely.

"I am spinning this fine thread," answered the woman. "Would you like to try?" And she held the spindle out to the curious girl.

"*Oh!*" cried the Princess. As she took the spindle, she pricked her finger and immediately fell asleep.

At the same moment, everyone in the castle fell asleep. The King and the Queen slept in the throne room. The servants slept in the hall. Even the cook and the kitchen dogs fell into a deep sleep.

Many, many years later ~ exactly one hundred, in fact ~ a Prince happened to be passing the castle. It was so overgrown with brambles that you could only see the topmost turrets. But as he rode along beside the high, thorny hedge, the Prince saw something magical. Suddenly, the hedge burst into bloom! A thousand roses spread their petals in the sunshine, and the hedge opened to let the Prince through.

The Prince was astonished to see all the sleepers in the castle. At last, he found himself in the small room where the Princess herself was sleeping. He was so dazzled by her beauty that he bent over and kissed her.

At that moment, the hundred years came to an end. The Princess opened her eyes, and the first thing she saw was a handsome young man, smiling down at her. Gently, he led her from the room to the courtyard below, where the whole castle was coming to life.

It was not long before the Prince and Princess were married, and the King once more gave a great feast. But this time, he was very careful indeed with his invitations!

THE FROG PRINCE

Once upon a time, there was a King who had seven beautiful daughters. The youngest was the loveliest of them all.

On sunny days, the youngest Princess loved to play with her golden ball in a shady wood beside the castle. The sunlight sparkled through the leaves onto a cool pool nearby.

One day, when the Princess threw her golden ball high into the air, something dreadful happened. It fell ... SPLASH! ... into the water and sank to the bottom.

"It is lost forever!" the girl cried, but a croaky voice interrupted her.

"I could dive down and find your ball," said a little green frog by the pool, "if you would promise that I could be your friend, and share your meals, and snuggle into your little bed at night."

"Anything!" gasped the Princess hastily.

SPLISH! The frog dived into the water and soon reappeared with the golden ball.

The Princess was so delighted that she forgot all about her promise. She ran straight back to the palace, ignoring the little voice calling from the wood.

That evening, the King and his family sat down to supper. Just as they were about to start their meal, there came a croaking sound at the door. The youngest Princess tried to ignore it, but the King noticed that she looked pale.

"Who is there?" he asked.

Then the Princess explained about her promise. "But I can't let a horrible frog share my supper," she cried.

"A promise is a promise, my dear," said the King. "Let us meet your friend."

So, although the Princess shuddered every time she looked at him, the frog was allowed onto the table to share her supper.

After supper, the Princess tried to slip off to bed by herself.

"What about me?" croaked a little voice from the table. The Princess tried to pretend that she had not heard, but the King gave her a stern look.

"Remember what I said about promises," he said.

The Princess unwillingly carried the frog to her bedroom and put him down in a corner.

"I'd much rather sit on your pillow," croaked the little green creature.

Close to tears, the Princess picked up the frog and dropped him onto her pillow.

At once, the little green frog disappeared! In his place sat a handsome, smiling Prince.

"Don't be afraid," he said. "A wicked witch put a spell on me that only a kind Princess could break. I hope that we can still be friends, now that I am no longer a frog."

From that moment, the Prince and Princess became the very best of friends. In fact, a few years later, they had a wonderful wedding, and did not forget to invite some very special little green guests to join the celebrations.

THE FISHERMAN AND HIS WIFE

One sunny day, a poor fisherman caught a very fine fish. He was just about to unhook it from his line, when something odd happened.

"Please wait a moment," said the fish.

The fisherman rubbed his eyes. A fish that talked! He must be dreaming.

But the beautiful silvery fish explained, "I am not really a fish but an enchanted Prince. Please put me back in the water."

"Of course," said the fisherman. "I wouldn't dream of eating a talking fish!" He put the fish back in the sea and went home to his wife.

The fisherman and his wife lived in a rickety old hut near the beach. It was in a terrible state! Everything was higgledy piggledy, and the place had not been cleaned for a very long time.

When the fisherman told his wife about the talking fish, she cried out, "You silly man! You should have asked for something for us in return. Go straight back and ask for a nice little cottage to live in."

The next morning, the shoemaker and his wife could hardly wait to creep down into the workshop. Sure enough, there on the workbench were *two* pairs of dainty shoes.

"I've never seen such fine workmanship," gasped the shoemaker.

Once again, he had no trouble in selling the shoes for a very handsome price.

From that day onward, the shoemaker's troubles were ended. Each evening, he cut out leather to make several pretty pairs of shoes. Each morning, he found the shoes standing ready on his workbench. Soon everyone knew where the finest shoes in town were to be found, and the shoemaker's shop was busy from morning till night.

One day, near Christmas, as the shoemaker closed the door on his last customer, his wife said, "I've been thinking, my dear, that we should try to find out who has been helping us all this time."

The shoemaker agreed. That night, instead of going to bed, he and his wife hid behind the workbench and waited to see what would happen.

As the clock struck midnight, the door opened and in danced two little men. They were dressed in rags and their feet were bare, but they cheerfully sat down and began to sew. Before dawn, they had finished their work and slipped out into the street.

"So now we know," smiled the shoemaker. "What funny little men!"

"But did you notice, my dear, how old and torn their clothes were?" asked his wife. "Surely, the least we can do to thank them is to make them some new trousers, shirts and stockings. And you could make them some little shoes."

A few nights later, the tiny presents were finished. The shoemaker and his wife laid them on the workbench and hid as before.

Just after midnight, the little men reappeared. At the sight of the clothes waiting for them, they danced with happiness.

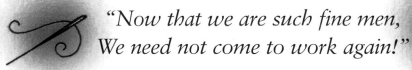

"Now that we are such fine men,
We need not come to work again!"

they sang, and they skipped out of the shop, never to return.

The shoemaker and his wife were happy and wealthy for the rest of their days, but they never forgot the two little elves who gave them a helping hand.

THE MUSICIANS OF BREMEN

Once there was a donkey who worked very hard for his master. But when he became old and tired, he could no longer carry such large loads, and it became clear that his master would not keep him for much longer.

"The best thing for me to do," thought the donkey, "would be to take myself off before that day comes. I shall go to Bremen and become a musician. My braying has often been noticed."

So early one morning, the donkey set off for Bremen. On the way, he met a dog, sheltering by a tumbledown wall.

"You look rather sorry for yourself, old friend," said the donkey.

"I am too old to go hunting with my master," growled the dog. "Now, he hardly feeds me at all."

"Come with me to Bremen!" laughed the donkey. "If I bray and you bark, we shall make fine music!"

Off went the donkey and the dog. Before long, they met a cat, crouched on a roof.

"It's a fine morning!" called the donkey. But the cat meowed pitifully.

"Maybe it is for you," she called, "but I am old and even the mice laugh at me."

"Come with us and be a musician!" called the donkey and the dog. "Your voice is still strong and tuneful."

So the donkey and the dog and the cat went on their way to Bremen, singing as they went.

Now the musicians were making a very loud noise, but as they passed by a farmer's barn, they heard a noise that was so loud, it drowned even their strange and wonderful singing.

"Cock-a-doodle-doo! Cock-a-doodle-doo!"

"Goodness me," said the donkey. "This is a strange time of day for a rooster to be crowing."

"What else can I do?" called the rooster. "The farmer is having some friends to dinner tonight. I'm very much afraid that I'm the main course!"

"Don't worry," the donkey replied. "I can think of a much better use for your voice. You just come along with us."

And so the donkey and the dog and the cat and the rooster went on toward Bremen.

By the evening, the animals were tired. They needed a warm place to sleep and a fine dinner to end the day. At last, in the distance, they saw the lighted window of a little cottage.

When they reached it, the rooster flew up and looked in the window.

"I can see four robbers, sitting down to a delicious meal!" he called.

"That sounds just right for us," said the donkey. "And what is more, I have a plan."

So the dog climbed on the donkey's back. And the cat climbed on the dog's back. And the rooster perched on the cat's back. Then the animals went right up to the window and sang their music at the tops of their voices. It was an extraordinary sound!

"It's a ghost!" cried one robber, and rushed from the room.

"It's a goblin!" cried another, scrambling after him as fast as he could.

"It's a troll!" called the third, stumbling over his chair.

"I want my mother!" sobbed the last robber. "Wait for me!"

In just a few minutes, the four animal friends had taken the robbers' places at the table and were enjoying a delicious meal.

Later that night, the animals slept soundly in the warm, comfortable cottage. But the robbers had talked themselves out of their fear and crept back to see if the coast was clear. Luckily, the dog's sharp ears heard them coming, so the animals hid behind the door and waited silently in the darkness.

As soon as the robbers were inside the cottage, the donkey cried, "Now!" and took hold of one robber's trousers with his strong yellow teeth. In a flash, the dog had fastened his jaws around the second robber's ankles. The cat had jumped and sunk her claws into the third robber's shoulder. And the rooster had pecked the nose of the fourth robber so hard that it was never the same again.

Well, those robbers ran away even faster than they had the first time, leaving the four friends in peace. The cottage was so charming that they never did reach Bremen, but they made time for their singing practice every day. And if you had ever heard them, you would know that the good people of Bremen had a very lucky escape indeed!

LITTLE RED RIDING HOOD

Once there was a little girl who lived on the edge of a huge forest. The person she loved most in all the world was her grandmother, whose cottage was further along the forest path. One day, the old lady sent her granddaughter a beautiful red cape with a hood. The little girl loved it so much that she would *not* take it off! So that was why everyone called her Little Red Riding Hood.

One morning, Little Red Riding Hood's mother heard that the grandmother was not feeling well.

"Run along the forest path with this basket of food, Little Red Riding Hood," she said. "Your grandmother will feel better as soon as she sees you."

In no time at all, the little girl was ready to set off. She was wearing her red cape, of course.

"Now just remember," warned her mother, "you must go straight there and don't stop for *anything*."

"Don't worry," Little Red Riding Hood smiled, and off she went.

Now Little Red Riding Hood had not gone very far down the path, when out of the trees stepped a very large wolf!

"Why, Little Red Riding Hood," he said, "where are you off to in such a hurry?"

The little girl answered politely, "I am going to see my grandmother, but I'm afraid I *cannot* stop to talk." And on she went.

But when she was halfway to her grandmother's house, Little Red Riding Hood was surprised to see the same wolf leaning against a tree.

"I was just thinking, dear child," he said, "how nice it would be to take your grandmother some of the beautiful flowers that bloom by the path."

Well, that did seem to be a good idea, so Little Red Riding Hood stopped to gather the flowers. And when she looked up, the wolf was gone.

It was rather late by the time that Little Red Riding Hood knocked on her grandmother's door.

"Come in!" called a gruff voice.

"Poor grandmother, you don't sound well at all," cried the little girl.

Inside the cottage, Little Red Riding Hood tiptoed toward her grandmother's bed. The old lady did not *look* very well either!

"Why grandmother," gasped her granddaughter, not very politely, "what big ears you have!"

"The better to hear you with!" croaked the invalid.

Little Red Riding Hood crept closer still.

"Oh grandmother, what big eyes you have!" she cried in surprise.

"The better to see you with!" growled the figure in the big bed.

Little Red Riding Hood took one more step and had a dreadful shock.

"Oh grandmother, what big teeth you have!"

"The better to eat you with!" roared the wolf, jumping from the bed!

But just as the wolf was about to eat Little Red Riding Hood up in one enormous bite, a passing huntsman, who had heard the noise, rushed into the cottage.

"Aha!" he cried. "I've been looking for you, Mr. Wolf! Wait till I lay my hands on you!" And he chased the wolf right out of the cottage and into the trees.

Little Red Riding Hood was just recovering from her shock, when she heard a muffled sound from the cupboard. Bravely, she flung open the doors.

"Oh grandmother!" she cried with relief. "I thought you had been eaten up by that wicked wolf."

"He was saving me for dessert," said the old lady, hugging her granddaughter.

"And how are you feeling?" asked the little girl, remembering that her grandmother was not well.

"I *always* feel better when I see you, Little Red Riding Hood," smiled her grandmother. "You must know that!"

Several hours later, Snow White was awoken by a sharp little voice.

"Just what do you think you are doing in our house?" it asked.

Snow White looked up to see seven dwarfs, in working clothes, standing around. The young girl took her courage in both hands and explained what had happened to her.

"And now," she said, "I have nowhere to go at all."

"Yes, you do!" chorused the dwarfs. "You can stay here with us!" They told her that they worked all day and needed someone to look after them.

"You will be safe here," they said. "But you must promise us never to open the door to a stranger."

So Snow White stayed
with the dwarfs. She cooked
their meals and cared for
their little house, but her life
was very different from the
one she had lived at home.
She longed for someone to
talk to during the long days.

Then, one fine morning,
her wish came true. An old woman, with a basket of
pretty things, knocked on the cottage door.

Snow White longed to look through the laces and
ribbons in the stranger's basket, but she remembered
her friends' warning. Still, she could not resist talking
to the woman through the open window.

Snow White did not realize that her visitor was none other than the wicked Queen in disguise. For months, the Queen had been so happy that she did not consult her mirror at all. When she did, she had a terrible shock.

"O Queen, you cannot have your will,
For Snow White is the fairest still."

Raging through her kingdom, the Queen had hunted high and low for the missing girl, taking on different disguises. She could scarcely hide her delight at finding her at last.

"You are wise not to open the door to strangers, my dear," she smiled. "But to show that there are no hard feelings, please take this shiny red apple as a gift from a new friend."

It seemed impolite to refuse, so Snow White stretched out her hand and took the apple. It looked delicious. Waving goodbye to her visitor, she took one tiny bite.

When the dwarfs returned from their work that evening, they found Snow White lying lifeless on the floor, the apple still clutched in her hand.

"This is the work of the Queen, I'm sure," cried one dwarf, sobbing. "She has robbed us of the sweetest girl in the world."

Sadly, the dwarfs took their friend and placed her in a crystal coffin, taking turns to watch over her night and day. She seemed to grow more lovely as she lay there, silent, cold and still.

One morning, a young Prince rode by and saw the coffin and the beautiful girl inside. He fell in love with her at once and vowed, although she could never be his bride, that he would not be parted from her.

"Let me take her back to my palace," he begged, "where she can lie in state as befits a Princess."

The dwarfs discussed the matter and agreed that she deserved no less. Carefully, they helped the Prince to lift the coffin.

But as they did so, the piece of apple that had caught in Snow White's throat was dislodged. She took one breath and then another. Amid the tears of her friends, she sat up and smiled at the Prince.

You may guess the end of the story. Snow White and her Prince lived happily ever after. And the wicked Queen? She was so eaten up with rage and envy that she died soon after, leaving the young couple to enjoy their happiness in peace.

RAPUNZEL

Once there lived a man and wife who wanted very much to have a child of their own. But year after year passed, and they did not have a baby. Often, the woman would sit sadly looking out of the window, from which she could see the garden next door.

Now this garden was very beautiful, full of flowers and vegetables, but no one dared to enter it because it belonged to a witch. One day, as the woman looked out, she suddenly had a great longing to eat one of the lettuces growing below.

"I feel as though I shall die if I do not have one of those delicious lettuces," she said to her husband. And she looked so pale and anxious that the poor man, much against his better judgment, agreed to go down and fetch her a lettuce.

That evening, as it was getting dark, the man crept over the wall and hurried toward the vegetable garden. He was just about to cut a beautiful lettuce when a voice crackled through the twilight.

"How dare you come into my garden to steal from me?"

The husband nearly jumped out of his skin. It was the witch! Stuttering with fright, he explained about his wife's great craving for lettuce.

"Very well," laughed the witch, "I'm not an unreasonable woman. You may take a lettuce, if you will give me your firstborn child in return."

The man was so frightened that he would have agreed to anything. And besides, he did not think that it was very likely that he would have children now, so he mumbled his thanks, took the lettuce, and ran.

But the strange thing was that only a few months later his wife gave birth to a beautiful baby daughter. Despite the pleadings of the mother and father, the witch made the man keep his promise. She took the child at once and gave her the name Rapunzel.

The little girl grew quickly and became more lovely every day. The witch was very kind to her and treated her like her own child, except for one thing. When Rapunzel was twelve years old, the witch took her to a high tower and put her in a room at the very top. There was no door and no stairs ~ just a small window for Rapunzel to look out from.

When the witch wished to visit, she stood at the bottom of the tower and called out,

"Rapunzel, Rapunzel,
Let down your hair!"

At this, the girl would lower her long, braided hair from the window, and the witch would climb up.

A few years later, a Prince came riding past and heard a beautiful voice singing from the top of the tower. Puzzled, he hid behind some bushes and waited to see what would happen. Of course, before long, the witch visited Rapunzel in her usual way.

As soon as the witch had gone, the Prince came out of his hiding place and called out,

"Rapunzel, Rapunzel,
Let down your hair!"

Thinking that the witch had returned, Rapunzel did as she was asked. She was astonished to see a tall, handsome young man climbing through the high window instead.

"Don't be afraid," he said. "I heard your beautiful singing and longed to see you for myself. Now I know that you are as lovely as your voice."

The Prince spoke kindly to the girl and, as she grew to know him, she grew to love him.

All went well until one day when the witch was
visiting. As she climbed into the tower, Rapunzel
spoke without thinking.

"Why is it, Mother dear, that you feel so much
heavier than the Prince does, when he climbs up?"

There was an awful silence. Then the witch flew
into such a rage that the stones of the tower trembled.
She took out some scissors and snipped off Rapunzel's
long braid. With her magic powers, she banished the
frightened girl to a desert far away. Then, as the sun
went down, she crouched near the window and waited.

Before long, a voice drifted up from below.

"Rapunzel, Rapunzel,
Let down your hair!"

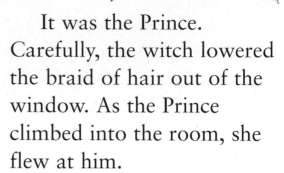

It was the Prince. Carefully, the witch lowered the braid of hair out of the window. As the Prince climbed into the room, she flew at him.

"I wanted to keep my darling safe from such as you!" she spat. And with a huge push, she hurled him to the ground.

The Prince fell like a stone into some bushes at the foot of the tower. He managed to stagger to his feet, but his eyes had been scratched by thorns, and he could not see at all. In darkness as black as his despairing thoughts, he stumbled away to a life of ceaseless wandering.

Years later, the Prince came to the desert where Rapunzel was living. In the distance, he heard a sound he thought that he would never hear again. It was the sweetest voice in the world, singing sadly.

"Rapunzel!" cried the Prince, running forward. The poor girl was so overjoyed that she covered his face with kisses and tears. As they fell onto the Prince's eyes, the tears healed his wounds. Once more he could see the girl he loved.

The Prince and Rapunzel returned to his kingdom, where they lived happily together for the rest of their days. The witch has never been heard of since ~ but it would be wise never to take as much as a petal, the next time you visit a beautiful garden.

THE TWELVE DANCING PRINCESSES

There was once a King who had twelve beautiful daughters. It was not easy having so many girls to keep an eye on, so the King made sure that he could rest peacefully at night by locking his daughters into their room. But every morning, when he came to unlock the door, he found the girls sleeping as though exhausted and twelve pairs of dancing shoes worn out on the floor.

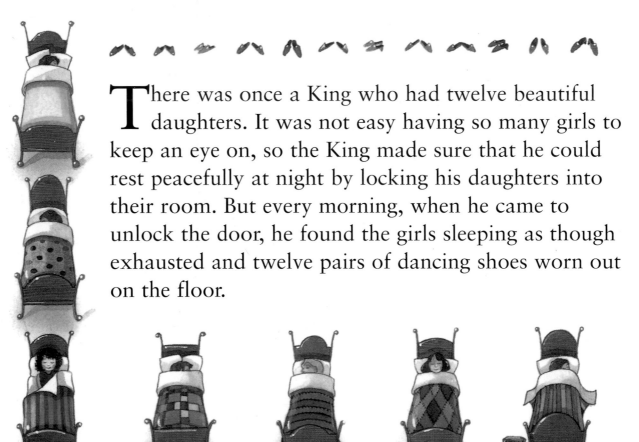

The King could not
understand it. The more
he thought about it, the
more worried he
became. At last he
made a royal
proclamation that
whoever could solve
the mystery might
choose one of the
girls to be his wife
and become heir to
the throne. But if, after
three nights, the suitor
was no nearer to the truth,
then he must lose his life.

Several Princes came to try. They took up their
posts in the hallway outside the Princesses' room and
waited to see who came in. But one by one, they fell
asleep and saw nothing at all. And one by one, they
lost their heads.

KING THROSTLEBEARD

There was once a King who had a very beautiful daughter. Although she was the loveliest girl in the whole kingdom, and queues of suitors presented themselves every year, her heart was cold and proud. She laughed at all of them and sent them away.

"Very well," said her father, "I will sort this out once and for all. I will invite every eligible nobleman from far and near to a great feast. When you see them together, you are sure to find someone that you like."

So every King, Prince, Duke, Marquis, Earl and Baron came from hundreds of miles around. They were lined up in the great hall, and the Princess walked up and down the rows looking at them each in turn, like a general inspecting his troops!

"Ho, ho, ho! Look at his skinny legs!" she laughed, as she passed one very learned Prince.

"Ha, ha, ha! He looks like a frog!" she giggled, as she looked down at a very kind and hardworking Duke.

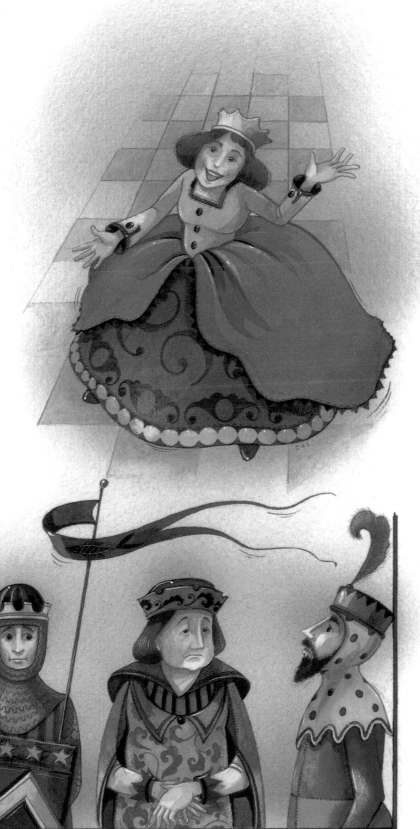

It was the same all the way down the line, until she came to a young King who was charming in every way. Still, there was something about his face that reminded the Princess of a bright-eyed bird.

"I'll call you King Throstlebeard," she chuckled. "I couldn't possibly marry someone so birdbrained! Ha, ha,ha!"

Seeing that she had rejected every suitor in the most unkind way, the Princess's father soon grew very angry with her.

"You will marry the first beggar who comes to the palace gates," he declared. "Then you will be sorry."

A few days later, a strolling player sat below the King's window and sang a haunting song. The King at once asked for him to be brought into the castle.

"Your singing has brought you a greater reward than you could imagine," he said. "Here is my daughter. She shall be your wife."

Despite the Princess's protests, she was married at once, and ushered out of the palace to make her way in the world with her new husband.

The Princess and the beggar trudged along through some beautiful countryside. The Princess wondered whose land could be so pleasing. Her husband laughed and replied,

"King Throstlebeard owns all both far and near. You could have shared in everything that's here."

Then the Princess began to wish that she had not been so hasty. But it was too late now.

All day they walked along, and everywhere there were fine towns and well-tended farms. Each time she asked, the beggar told the Princess that all of this belonged to King Throstlebeard.

"I have been a fool," moaned the Princess. "If only I had married him!"

At this, the beggar became angry.

"You have been married to me for less than a day," he said, "and already you are wishing for another husband. Am I so unworthy of you?"

Before she could reply, the Princess saw that they had stopped at a tiny hut.

"This is my home," the beggar told his wife, "where you and I shall live together."

"But where do the servants live?" she asked.

"What servants?" chuckled the beggar. "You will be doing all the work around here, my dear."

So the Princess's new life began, but things did not go smoothly. She was no good at cooking or cleaning or washing the clothes. She could not make baskets or spin thread.

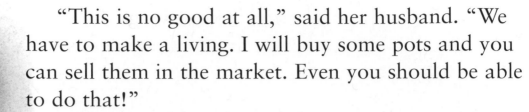

"This is no good at all," said her husband. "We have to make a living. I will buy some pots and you can sell them in the market. Even you should be able to do that!"

"But someone who knows me might see me!" wailed the Princess.

"So they might," replied her husband with a smile.

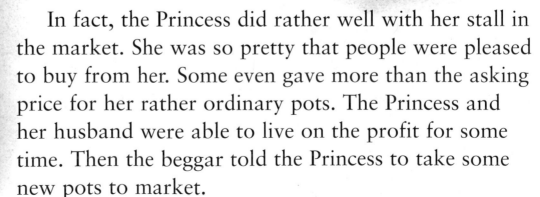

In fact, the Princess did rather well with her stall in the market. She was so pretty that people were pleased to buy from her. Some even gave more than the asking price for her rather ordinary pots. The Princess and her husband were able to live on the profit for some time. Then the beggar told the Princess to take some new pots to market.

This time, things did not go so well. The Princess set up her stall on a corner. Before an hour had passed, a runaway horse crashed into the stall and broke every pot that she had.

Of course, the Princess's husband was furious.

"You are completely useless," he said. "I cannot afford to keep you. But there is a post for a kitchen maid at the palace. They will feed you and you can bring home some scraps for me too."

All day long, the Princess, who had once been so proud, was up to her elbows in dishwater. Soon, she had to work even harder than ever, because a great feast was being held at the palace.

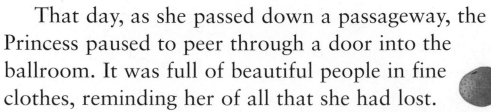

That day, as she passed down a passageway, the Princess paused to peer through a door into the ballroom. It was full of beautiful people in fine clothes, reminding her of all that she had lost.

"It is my own fault," she admitted. "If I had not been so proud, I could have led a wonderful life."

At that moment, the King came into the room. To the Princess's horror, she realized that it was King Throstlebeard, whom she had rejected. Yet the King came straight toward the pretty girl and swept her, rags and all, into the dance. As he did so, the jars of scraps that she had saved fell out of the Princess's pockets and rolled across the floor.

The whole company roared with laughter at the sight, while the poor girl wished that the floor would open and swallow her up.

As she fled from the ballroom, the Princess found her way blocked by a man at the door. To her amazement, this was also King Throstlebeard!

"Don't be afraid," he said kindly. "I have taken on many forms, including the beggar whom you married. I see that you have learned to give up your pride and coldness. Now I am proud to make you my Queen."

From that day forward, the new Queen was the happiest woman in the world, and her kindness to everyone was known throughout the land.

RUMPELSTILTSKIN

Once upon a time, there was a miller who was very proud of his family. But he was not a very sensible man, as you will see.

One day, it was the miller's turn to appear before the King and account for his year's work in the royal mill. Everything went well until the end of the interview. Before dismissing the miller, the King asked about his family.

"I hear that you have a very pretty daughter," said the King.

"Not just pretty, Your Majesty," cried the miller with pride. "Why, she is the cleverest girl in the kingdom as well!"

"Really?" said the King. "Tell me, what can she do that is so clever?"

"She ... she ... she ... can spin straw into gold!" blurted out the foolish miller. He had said the very first thing that came into his head.

The King looked hard at the miller. He was very fond of money. It seemed unlikely that the girl could do as her father said, but it was worth a try.

"Bring her to the palace," said the King. "And I mean *right* away!"

So the miller went home and fetched his daughter. The King could not help noticing that she was a very pretty girl, but his mind was full of visions of gleaming gold. He took the girl to a small room, containing a spinning wheel and a huge heap of straw.

"Spin that into gold before dawn," said the King, locking the door, "or it will be the worse for you."

The girl began to cry. She had no idea what to do. Suddenly, through her tears, she saw that she was no longer alone. A strange little man stood before her.

"I may be able to help you," he said with a crafty smile, "but, of course, I will need something from you in return."

The hope that had brightened the girl's eyes for a moment faded away. "I have nothing to give you," she said.

Her visitor's sharp little eyes twinkled greedily. "Your pretty glass necklace will be payment enough," he said, and at once he set to work.

While the poor girl cried herself to sleep, the little man worked at the spinning wheel. All night long, it whirred and hummed. Before dawn, the strange little man had vanished as suddenly as he had arrived.

When he opened the door, the King was amazed and delighted to see a pile of golden thread where the straw had been.

"Tonight," he said, "I will give you a larger pile of straw. We must test your skills again."

That night, the little man once again appeared to help the bewildered girl. This time, he took the ring from her finger as payment.

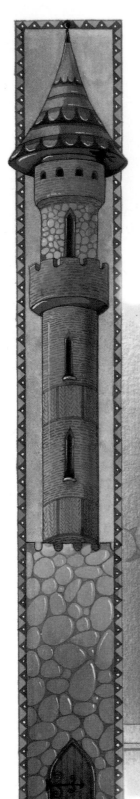

The King was a happy man. The next night, he showed the miller's daughter into an even larger room in a tower.

"If you complete your task again before morning," he said, "I will make you my Queen."

Once more, the strange little man appeared, but this time the poor girl sobbed her heart out.

"I have nothing left to give you," she explained. "Nothing at all."

The little man thought for a moment. "When you are Queen," he said, "you can give me your firstborn child instead."

What choice did the desperate girl have? Once again, the little man worked through the night.

The next morning, there was great rejoicing in the castle. The King announced his wedding to the pretty girl who had won his heart, and the miller was quite overcome with pride.

A year later, the happy young Queen rocked her first child gently in her arms. She was thinking only of the future. Suddenly, the strange little man of the year before appeared before her.

"I have come to remind you of your promise," he said.

The Queen begged him to take her jewels instead of her child, but the little man shook his head.

"I will give you one more chance," he grinned. "If you can guess my name before three nights have passed, you can keep your baby."

At once, the Queen sent out messengers to find the strangest names in the kingdom, and for the next two nights she tried every name she could think of ~ without success.

On the third night, a soldier came to her with an odd story.

"As I was riding through a wood," he said, "I saw a strange little man dancing around a fire and singing:

'The Queen can never win my game,
Rumpelstiltskin is my name!'"

That night, when the little man appeared, the Queen said, "Is your name Hibblehob?"

"No!" he yelled.

"Is it Grigglegreggers?"

"No, no, no!"

"Well, is it... Rumpelstiltskin?"

The little man went red in the face. He whizzed around and around in fury and stamped his foot so hard that he disappeared right through the floor!

And, you know, no one has seen that strange little man from that day to this.